Wilderness Cat

Wilderness Cat

by NATALIE KINSEY-WARNOCK

illustrated by MARK GRAHAM

COBBLEHILL BOOKS / Dutton · New York

To my sister, Helen   NKW

To Diane and Katy   MG

Library of Congress Cataloging-in-Publication Data
Kinsey-Warnock, Natalie.
Wilderness cat / Natalie Kinsey-Warnock ;
illustrated by Mark Graham.
p.   cm.
Summary: When Serena's family moves fifty miles to a
wilderness area in Canada, they think that they have left their
cat Moses behind, but then they receive a surprise visitor.
ISBN 0-525-65068-7
[1. Cats—Fiction.   2. Frontier and pioneer life—Fiction.
3. Canada—Fiction.]   I. Graham, Mark, 1952- ill.   II. Title.
PZ7.K6293Wil   1991   [E]—dc20   90-24250   CIP   AC

Published in the United States by Cobblehill Books,
an affiliate of Dutton Children's Books,
a division of Penguin Books USA Inc.,
375 Hudson Street, New York, New York 10014
Typography by Kathleen Westray
Printed in Hong Kong   First Edition

10 9 8 7 6 5 4 3 2 1

$\mathcal{M}$ama's voice rang through the darkness of the cabin.

"Hurry, girls. Your papa wants to get an early start."

Hannah jumped out of bed, but Serena patted the black cat sleeping on the quilt.

"Get up, Moses. We are moving to Canada!"

Serena and Hannah ate their mush while Papa and Luke loaded the cart. Papa put in his ax, the iron kettle, and bags of cornmeal, beans, and flour. Papa would build beds, chairs, and a table in their new home. Mama packed her dishes in the linens and quilts. Last to go in was the dirt-filled tub of lilac bushes and the moss rose that Grandmother Elkins had brought from Scotland.

"Ready to go, Ruthie?" Papa asked Mama. Mama nodded.
Serena picked up Moses.

"You will like it in Canada," she told him.

Papa looked at Mama and sighed.

"We cannot take Moses to Canada," Papa said. "A cat does not like to ride in a cart. Moses would only jump out and run away into the woods. And fifty miles is too far for him to walk. We will leave Moses with the Andersons and get another cat in Canada."

"I don't want another cat," Serena cried. "I want Moses."

"There will be no more outbursts," Papa said sternly. "Take him over there now."

Mrs. Anderson opened the door when Serena knocked. Two small children peeked around her skirt.

"We shall be happy to have a fine cat like Moses," she said kindly. Serena gave Moses to Mrs. Anderson and ran home as fast as she could so Mrs. Anderson would not see her cry.

For four days, Papa, Mama, Luke, Serena, and Hannah traveled through the wilderness to Canada. The cart bumped and rattled over stones and logs. The trees grew so tall and thick that they hardly saw the sun.

At night, they camped next to streams where the tired horse could drink and eat grass that grew along the banks. As Serena lay under the stars, she tried not to think of Moses.

One afternoon, they came to a little house in a clearing.

"Here be your new home, Ruthie," Papa said.

Before they had moved, Papa had traveled to Canada to pick out
good land for farming. He had cut trees, planted some vegetables,
and built a shanty on the bank of a river.

Canada was an exciting place to live. There were no neighbors nearby, and Serena heard wolves at night. But she missed Moses.

Sometimes St. Francis Indians came by the shanty. They would throw some ducks on the floor and by motions with their hands give Mama to understand that they wanted potatoes. Mama would open the door to the root cellar and motion for them to help themselves. Sometimes the Indians brought venison or fish without asking anything in return.

Mama was scared of the Indians, but Serena liked them. They looked fierce with their sharp knives, but they were kind and once brought her a necklace of bear claws.

Papa often went hunting and fishing with the Indians, but sometimes he came home empty-handed.

Serena knew Papa worried how he would feed them all. He hadn't known life in Canada would be so hard. Three times that winter, Papa walked back to Craftsbury to work and earn a bushel of cornmeal. He carried it home on his back, fifty long miles through the deep snow. One time he took Luke with him, to earn enough meal to see them through the winter.

The house seemed empty without Papa and Luke. Each
evening, Serena watched the path through the woods where they
would come.

One morning, there was no breakfast on the table when Serena and Hannah got up.

Serena looked in the cupboard. There was only a handful of meal left and two potatoes.

"We shall have breakfast and dinner together," Mama said cheerfully.

Mama made cornmeal mush and baked the potatoes for Serena and Hannah. She did not take any for herself.

"You can have mine, Mama," Serena said slowly.

"That's my brave girl," Mama said. "But no. You eat it."

Snow fell all afternoon, and the wind howled like wolves.

There was nothing to eat for supper, and Hannah cried herself to sleep.

"Will we starve, Mama?" Serena asked.

"No," said Mama. "Go to bed now. The Lord will provide."

Serena dreamed of Moses. He was crying for her, so loudly it seemed real.

She opened her eyes and listened. Something *was* crying outside.

Serena ran to open the door. Moses meowed and curled around her legs. He was very thin from weeks of struggling through the deep snow, and there was a piece of one ear missing, but it was Moses.

"Mama! Mama!" Serena screamed. "It's Moses! Look what he brought!"

A large white snowshoe hare lay on the doorstep. Mama threw up her hands when she saw it, and tears filled her eyes.

Mama skinned the hare and set it to roast in the fireplace. Serena and Hannah watched while it sizzled and sputtered. Suddenly the door burst open.

"I smelled that meat a mile away," Papa's voice boomed out. "Ruth, how did you ever manage it?"

Papa and Luke listened while Serena told of finding Moses and the hare on the step. Papa shook his head.

"I never heard of such a thing," he said. "Mrs. Anderson sent some potatoes. She said Moses disappeared soon after we left last summer."

"The Lord sent us that cat," Mama said.

They had a glorious feast, meat and potatoes and golden cornbread baked over the fire. And Mama cut the meat into six pieces, one for each of them and one piece for Moses.

After supper, Moses washed himself from head to toe. He curled up on Serena's and Hannah's bed and sighed a long, contented sigh.

Suddenly, Serena had an awful thought.

"Mama, will we ever have to move again?"

"We may, someday," Mama said.

"Will we have to leave Moses?"

"No," Mama said firmly. "We'll never leave Moses behind."

Serena and Hannah climbed into bed and snuggled under the covers, with Moses between them. The wind howled outside, but Serena felt safe and warm. Papa and Mama were there to watch over her, there was food to eat, and Moses had come home.